Ninja Pug

Retrieving the Stolen Books

Amma Lee

INTRODUCTION

For Hanzo, an old man and successor to a Japanese ninja clan, lonely days came to an end when he took in Jiro. Jiro is Hanzo's only companion. They do everything and go everywhere together, but Jiro has a secret. Every morning when Hanzo trains using his ninja skills, Jiro watches him intently soaking in Hanzo's every move and technique. When Hanzo is gone or asleep, Jiro practices everything he's learned from Hanzo. The surprising twist is that Jiro is a dog, a small pug to be exact!

Since Hanzo was the last of his family after losing his only son, Ichiro, in a car accident and his grandson, Ryoichi, who went missing shortly after, Jiro has made it his duty to become Hanzo's successor! But Hanzo's world seems to go downhill fast once their home is broken into and some important books were discovered missing. Not wanting the old man to suffer any more than he has, Jiro decides to find Hanzo's missing books.

Jiro teams up with Luna, a white poodle, and they embark on a mission to retrieve Hanzo's books from the thieves. What the two small dogs were not expecting was that these books contain the power of the Hakumoto Clan. What is even more surprising is that the thieves happened to be highly talented and trained ninjas. Jiro's life is instantly turned upside down as secrets are revealed and someone from Jiro's past might have come back into his' and Hanzo's life. Follow Jiro and Luna on their journey in "Ninja Pug: Retrieving the Stolen Books."

CHAPTER ONE

"Time to rise and shine!" a loud explosion of barks woke Hanzo out of his deep sleep. Opening his old eyes, Hanzo looked down towards the foot of his bed to see little Jiro, his brown pug, wagging his tail happily.

"Good morning, Jiro," Hanzo said, lifting himself up out of his bed. Since Jiro woke Hanzo up, it must be 5:00 a.m. "I'm not as young as I use to be, but I at the very least make time to practice."

"Morning!" Jiro barked and jumped off of the bed. He followed his owner and waited for Hanzo patiently when he went to the bathroom. When the old man was done, Hanzo and Jiro made their way downstairs.

I thought he'd never wake up! Jiro thought to himself as he followed behind Hanzo. Jiro looked forward to watching his owner train every morning. The old Japanese man may not have been as young and vibrant as he used to be, but his ability to train and perform his Japanese katas and Kobudo was still top notch!

"Kyah!" Hanzo yelled as he made a tight fist and punched into the punching bag. Punch, kick, chop, punch, kick, chop. Jiro watched intensely as Hanzo gave the punching bag a piece of his mind. His movements were fast, despite his old age. Jiro respected Hanzo as an owner and as a friend. Though Jiro could speak and understand Hanzo, unfortunately, Hanzo couldn't translate Jiro's speech.

"Now do your famous spinning kick!" Jiro called out jumping up, and Hanzo smiled.

"Easy Jiro," his kind voice resonated throughout the small basement. "You're barking too loud. It may just be you and me, but think of the neighbors." Jiro sat down and whined. Jiro was excited to watch Hanzo practice, but he could hear the sadness in the older man's voice when he said it was just him and Jiro.

Jiro could tell that Hanzo was lonely. Hanzo had no family other than Jiro. Hanzo had lost his only son, Ichiro, in a car accident, and his grandson, Ryoichi, had gone missing after the car crash. It's been many years since then, and police have given up the search for Ryoichi. Jiro knew that Hanzo was suffering from this every day.

"Are you thinking about them too?" Hanzo came over to Jiro and petted him on his head. Even though Hanzo could not understand Jiro, he could always somehow guess what Jiro was thinking. "I miss them, my son and grandson, but they're not here anymore. I can't hold onto the past, but you are here with me and always have been. One of the best days of my life was when I brought you home to live with me." Jiro listened to Hanzo's words and barked out his satisfaction of them being said to him.

Jiro and Hanzo have been together since Ichiro passed away. Hanzo found the little guy out on the street in the cold. Saddened by the fact that he had lost his only child, Hanzo decided to take the little guy home because he instantly felt a connection with the pug. Hanzo no longer was going to feel lonely with Jiro by his side. Jiro remembered that day like the back of his paw.

"Heh, sometimes when I look at you watching me so intensely, I think you understand what I'm doing," Hanzo said, going back to his training. When Hanzo wasn't looking, Jiro smiled exposing sharp small canine teeth. *Oh, you don't know the half of it*, Jiro thought to himself.

****

Jiro watched Hanzo train for two hours before the old man stopped. Hanzo went to freshen up and prepare him and Jiro something to eat.

"Right," Jiro said when his highly trained ears heard the sound of water running. Hanzo was in the shower, so Jiro had to make this quick. Standing up on his two back paws, Jiro walked over to the distinctly larger than him punching bag. "Kyah!" Jiro barked out and did a spinning kick into the punching bag. The punching bag didn't move as much because he wasn't as big or strong as Hanzo, but it moved.

Jiro had watched Hanzo train for years in the Japanese martial arts. Hanzo is in fact, a successor of a powerful Japanese ninja family. Since Hanzo had lost his family, Jiro made it his duty to become Hanzo's heir. "Kyah!" Jiro barked again and jumped high in the air and landed a powerful punch towards the upper half of the punching bag. For a dog, his skills were impressive. After years of watching Hanzo train, it wasn't surprising on how many of Jiro's moves mirrored Hanzo's.

"He should be calling me right about…" Jiro heard the shower being turned off from upstairs and he knew Hanzo more than likely had forgotten to bring in a towel. Jiro never understood why humans couldn't just shake themselves dry as he and other animals did.

"Jiro! Come here, boy!" Hanzo's voice resonated throughout the house. Jiro didn't waste any time running upstairs to Hanzo. He already knew what the man wanted, so Jiro made his way over to the laundry basket filled with clean laundry, and grabbed a towel out. "Good boy!" Jiro barked and made his way back downstairs. Hanzo would be another twenty minutes or so, so Jiro was going to practice some of the moves that he had seen Hanzo do.

"Humans' fists are stronger than dogs' paws, but I

shouldn't limit myself," Jiro mumbled to himself. Jiro remembered that Hanzo got into a slightly moving stance with his hands balled up into what Hanzo called the "monkey fist." Jiro ran around, never standing still for too long. This will confuse any opponent because they would never know what to expect. Since he couldn't ball up his paws, he made sure to press them tightly together. "Kyah!"

With all of his small body's might, Jiro jumped high into the air and punched the punching bag so hard that it fell back. Not wanting to make a lot a noise, Jiro quickly ran behind the bag and kicked it back into place. The small dog was breathing slightly hard, but he was happy with the progress that he had made. When he had first starting training, the punching bag didn't even flinch.

"Jiro!" Hanzo's voice resonated throughout the house. Jiro wanted to practice a little longer, but he didn't want to keep Hanzo waiting. Jiro barked and ran upstairs. Hanzo was in the kitchen preparing himself something to eat, Jiro walked over to his bowl, already knowing that the older man made sure to feed Jiro first.

Jiro wagged his tail happily as he ate his food. Hanzo came over to the small dog and rubbed his head.

"I'm so happy that you're still here, Jiro," Hanzo said looking lovingly at his precious dog. Jiro could hear the sadness in Hanzo's voice. It hurt to know that Hanzo was still suffering, but Jiro was happy that his presence offered the man some comfort. Once he was done cooking, Hanzo made his plate and sat down in front of Jiro's eating place.

Jiro finished his food quickly and turned around and watched Hanzo eat. Noticing Jiro's stare, Hanzo smiled and started talking to him. The old man talked about everything that came to his mind, he told jokes and laughed at his jokes. Jiro laughed too, even though he knew that Hanzo would just think that he was barking.

I want to do something for Hanzo. To make him more comfortable, Jiro thought to himself. Hanzo is so lonely, and Jiro knew that the old man needed some human companions. Jiro could only do so much as a dog. Jiro just didn't know what to do, but he had a weird feeling come over him. For some reason, Jiro felt that something was going to happen soon. Something that will change Hanzo's and Jiro's life.

CHAPTER TWO

"Throw the ball, Hanzo!" Jiro barked as he and Hanzo made their way back home. Hanzo was waving a small ball back and forth in his hand, and Jiro really wished that he would throw it already. They were coming back from the store and Hanzo was kind enough to buy Jiro a toy. If the toy was his, why won't he just throw it?

"Oh… you want the ball?" Hanzo teasingly asked Jiro and bent down a little to place the ball in front of Jiro's face. Jiro frowned. Hanzo enjoyed teasing Jiro because of how small he was, but the old man wasn't aware of the fact that Jiro's training has helped him jump higher. He never wanted to show off his ninja skills to Hanzo, but Jiro thought it was time to put Hanzo in his place.

"Check this out!" Jiro barked and jumped up towards Hanzo. Hanzo tried to hurriedly pull his hand away, but Jiro used his high jumping abilities to snatch the ball out of Hanzo's hand. Hanzo's eyes widened in shock, but his warm eyes lovingly looked at his dog friend.

"Hmmm…. when did you learn how to do that? Been watching me huh?" Hanzo asked, but he knew that he wasn't going to get a coherent response. Jiro howled in laughter. Jiro knew that Hanzo wasn't serious, but he was correct. He was this skilled in jumping because he had watched his oblivious sensei training every day.

Jiro started walking off in front of Hanzo feeling victorious. Hanzo spoke to Jiro like he was talking to a human and Jiro was happy for that. Jiro knew that the old man was his happiest when he was talking with Jiro. It didn't take long for the two of them to make it onto the street, and Jiro was getting anxious to get home. He knew Hanzo was going to take a nap for a few hours, and Jiro was looking forward to it. He'd be able to train without interruptions!

"Hmm?" Hanzo said pausing when they were outside of their fence. Jiro was deep in thought, but he focused his eyes when he noticed that Hanzo was acting strangely.

"What's wrong?" Jiro asking knowing full well that Hanzo wouldn't understand him. Hanzo's face looked weird, like he had tasted something sour. Jiro followed Hanzo's gaze towards the front door, and his eyes widened like small saucers. Someone had broken into their home!

"What?" Jiro questioned and ran towards the house.

"Jiro wait!" Hanzo called out when Jiro made a break towards the house. Jiro knew that Hanzo was worried about him, but Jiro was more concerned about what or who was in the house. Hanzo never hurt or bothered anyone, so why would someone break into their home? Jiro sniffed around and he could smell that someone had been in the house. Many of Hanzo's belongings were thrown on the floor, and Jiro could feel the anger rising in the pit of his stomach. He couldn't contain his anger, so he started growling. Not because someone was still in the house, but because someone had the nerve to do this to Hanzo.

"I don't sense anyone here, Jiro," Hanzo said from behind him. "It's okay, at least you and I was not in here when it happened," Hanzo said that, but Jiro could see the sadness lingering in his eyes. "Please be more careful as well, Jiro. What would I do if something happened to you?" Jiro looked up at Hanzo in surprised.

"What would I do if something happened to you?" Jiro responded, but Hanzo had already left out of the room to check on the rest of the house. Jiro growled one last time before following after Hanzo to check out the damage.

****

Hanzo spent a lot of time cleaning up the house. Whoever decided to break into their home, didn't appear to have taken anything. They didn't have much, so it wasn't a surprise that Hanzo didn't see anything was missing. Still though, just because nothing was taken, didn't mean that Jiro wasn't furious.

"Let's check the room," Hanzo said in his familiar sad voice. He mentioned a little while ago that he didn't want to bother the police with this minor break-in, but Jiro believed that Hanzo should call them so that the police could track down the perps. Whether they had stolen something or not, breaking into someone's home was still a crime.

The bedroom looked much like the rest of the house. Everything was thrown all over the place. Pictures were all over the floor, and all of Hanzo's drawers were opened with the contents thrown onto the floor. Still, even with all of the chaos, nothing appeared to have been missing. Slowly, Hanzo started putting things away.

"I can't believe this happened," Jiro growled, and Hanzo reached back behind him and petted the small dog's head.

"There isn't any danger here, boy. Everything is fine, just a couple of young hooligans messing around." Jiro growled again, not happy with what Hanzo said. How can someone be so calm in a situation like this? It was times like these when Jiro honestly could not understand Hanzo. "Wait…" Hanzo said pausing, and Jiro looked over the old man's shoulder to see what the problem was.

Hanzo looked around slowly at first, but then he started panicking. Hanzo then began desperately searching the room. *Was something missing after all?* Jiro thought to himself.

"What's wrong?" Jiro asked knowing full well Hanzo couldn't understand him. Jiro started pacing back and forth and began whining. Hanzo was in apparent distress, and Jiro didn't know why. He wished that Hanzo would tell him what was wrong.

"My books, some very special books were taken," Hanzo said sitting down slowly on the bed. He looked exhausted and equally heartbroken.

"Just some books?" Jiro asked perplexed. Jiro often saw Hanzo reading books, but out of all of the small things that could have been stolen with sentimental value, Jiro was shocked that books made Hanzo feel this way.

"Those books… they were important to me." Hanzo said sadly and sighed. Jiro could see how upset Hanzo was and Hanzo's sorrow was Jiro's as well. He might not have thought books going missing was important, but since it was important to Hanzo, he had no choice but to let them be important to him too. Hanzo stopped talking then to stop his sobs from escaping his lips and fell asleep.

"Tsk…" Jiro groaned walking out of the room. Whoever had broken into their house and stole Hanzo's books, he'll find them. He will find them and make them wish that they wouldn't have broken into their home. Hanzo was a powerful ninja, but he was old. Jiro knew that Hanzo would not try to track down the thieves and Hanzo surely wasn't going to get the police involved.

Going downstairs, Jiro walked over to the overly used punching bag and stared at it as if he was staring into the eyes of the thieves. "Whoever you are, big, small, old or young. I will find you. I will find you and take back what's rightfully Hanzo's. I may be a dog, but I am powerful enough to use my ninja and dog's skills to track you down."

Jiro jumped and punched the punching back hard enough to make the bag fall over. Usually, he would have tried his hardest to not make any noise, but he was angry. He trained hard for several hours as Hanzo slept. Jiro thought of ways to track down the culprits to bring them to justice, and he thought about all that needed to be done. It'll be hard since he's a dog and Jiro planned on going in without any backup, but he wasn't going to let that get the best of him.

It was time for him to put his training to good use.

CHAPTER THREE

Hanzo left early the next morning, but not without first fixing Jiro something to eat. Jiro was sad that Hanzo was leaving without him, but he was thankful that he was. Jiro had a lot to do, criminals to track down. He couldn't help the pain in his heart whenever he saw the sad look in Hanzo's eyes. Those books were important to the old man and Jiro was going to make sure that he got the books back.

Hanzo said that he would be out almost all day. Even for a dog, Jiro understood that Hanzo wouldn't be back until after dark. This was all the time that Jiro would need to at the very least track down the bothersome humans. Jiro ate his food and sniffed around the house. Hanzo didn't have any visitors, so it wasn't difficult to sniff out a scent that did not belong to Hanzo.

"From the smell of this scent, I believe at least two humans broke into the house," Jiro mumbled to himself. It was unfortunate that Hanzo wasn't as high-tech as other people with surveillance cameras littered around the small house, so he was working at a slight disadvantage. Jiro's nose was top-notch, but he wasn't as young as he used to be either. Hanzo didn't mind if Jiro went outside while he was gone as long as he didn't leave the yard. "Sorry, I'm going to have to disobey your orders today," Jiro said making his way outside.

"Jirooooo!" Luna, a white female poodle, called out once she saw the dog running through the yard with his face planted into the ground. It wasn't like Jiro disliked Luna or anything of that nature, but Luna got some very peculiar traits from her owner. Once she started talking, it was hard to get her to stop.

"Hi, Luna," Jiro said noticeably irritated. He didn't have time to hear Luna go on and on about her latest trip to the groomers. Jiro needed some clues to where the criminals may be.

"I see you're up and out early. You and the old man get into a fight? You bite up one of his…. shoes?" Luna asked once she remembered what humans called the things that they wear on their feet. She saw Hanzo leaving relatively early this morning, and it was rare to see Hanzo and Jiro not together.

"He went to take care of business. He's going to be out all day, so he was considerate enough to leave me at home." Jiro said rapidly and sniffed the air. Their scent was barely there, but Jiro was sure that he could still trail them. He didn't have a plan, he was more of a "plan as you go" type of dog. He was never the one to take the "safe route" into a situation. Not that he had ever been in a situation like this before.

Luna watched the small dog with amusement. She knew what he was doing, but she wanted to keep an eye on him a little longer before giving Jiro some information that might be of use to him and the old man. The two of them stopped talking until Luna couldn't take the silence any longer.

"I guess that you want to know about the humans that broke into your house?" Luna asked, and Jiro's head shot up as soon as the words left her mouth.

"Tell me what you know," Jiro said quickly, and Luna grinned exposing sharp little teeth.

"I will if you do me a favor," Luna responded. Jiro could feel in the pit of his stomach that he wasn't going to like the "favor" Luna had in mind.

****

"Are you sure it was just two of them?" Jiro asked once Luna told him everything that she knew of the burglary. Luna rolled her eyes and sighed.

"Of course I'm sure! Why would I make this up? I watched them enter the house and leave the house, and I only saw two people." *I already figured that there were two intruders, but it's good to know for sure*, Jiro thought to himself. What confused Jiro the most was the

15

fact that the break-in happened in the middle of the day. Jiro couldn't understand how there were no witnesses.

"What did they look like?" Jiro asked. Even though he could perfectly sniff the culprits out without knowing what they looked like, if he happened to see them on the street at least he would know them right away.

"They were young men. Humans would consider them teenagers. They were definitely Japanese, and they had some cloth over their mouths and a smaller piece of cloth wrapped around their heads." Luna responded, and Jiro looked at Luna in disbelief. Jiro was sure that he had seen something similar to Luna's description in movies. Was she telling him that ninjas broke into Hanzo's and his house?

"Ninjas," Jiro said positive that the culprits were ninjas. He wasn't aware of anyone in this day and age who were actually working as ninjas, and he doubted that the fact that Hanzo was the heir of a ninja family and them getting robbed by people described as ninjas was a coincidence. No, the thieves were ninjas, and apparently, someone tipped them off of Hanzo's history.

"Hmm… I believe my darling owner referred to people looking like them as ninjas in movies." Jiro nodded his head. He sniffed the ground near him again and turned around to follow the scent.

"Thanks for the information," Jiro said quickly trying to get away.

"Oh no you don't," Luna said jumping down from the porch. She had been bored these past few days, and she needed something to do. Luna only offered the information to Jiro if and only if he agreed to take her with him. Dangerous or not, she needed to get out of the house and the yard! Jiro sighed loudly.

"Fine, but you have to do everything that I say when I say it!" Jiro barked. This wasn't a mission for some ordinary dog, this was a mission for a ninja!

"Humph! Fine, I don't care." Luna said and walked out in front of him. Jiro looked at Luna slightly irritated. What type of skills did she bring to the table? From what Jiro could see, Luna was just your typical everyday poodle. If the situation did get dire, she wouldn't be able to defend herself. Still, if Luna had to go with him, she had to at least be able to be beneficial to Jiro.

"So, do you have any particular skills?" Jiro asked. The only thing the poodle appeared to be good at was yapping and being nosy.

"That's for me to know and you to discover!" Luna said and laughed. Jiro sighed again. *This is going to be a long day*, Jiro thought to himself. It was very rare that Hanzo left the house without Jiro, so if Jiro wanted to find Hanzo's missing books, then he'd need to do it today. Jiro thought about leaving at night, but he wasn't sure how soon he would get back. Hanzo went to sleep late and woke up early. Surely, Hanzo would notice the dog missing.

Jiro sniffed the air again trying to pick up the criminals' scent. He found it quickly and motioned for Luna to follow him.

"Come on, we have to wrap this up before Hanzo gets home," Jiro said.

"Humph, I don't like being told what to do, but I guess I'll listen this time," Luna said and took off as soon as Jiro made a dash in the direction where the criminals' scent was. Jiro looked slowly to his side , shocked that Luna was able to keep up with him. Even though they were both dogs, Jiro's ninja training should have still made it so that he was faster than Luna. This, however, wasn't the case.

Luna noticed Jiro's shock and looked over at him revealing small sharp teeth as she ran ahead of Jiro.

"Come on, Jiro! You got to keep up!" Luna said and managed to somehow outrun Jiro. Jiro was shocked for a moment, but then he smiled as well. *Looks like I underestimated her*, Jiro thought as he followed behind Luna. It didn't take the two of them too much time to find the building that reeked of the thieves' scent.

"This....doesn't look like a get in and get out type of place."

CHAPTER FOUR

Jiro and Luna looked at the apparently abandoned building, and something felt off.

"This is definitely the right place," Jiro mumbled mainly to himself. It was something about the building that made him feel weird. It almost felt like they were about to walk into something that was something so much more than what they would have ever dreamed.

"Yes, I'll have to agree with you on that one," Luna said nodding her head. Luna's small head moved from side to side as she sniffed the air around them. "This is definitely where the people who broke into your home are," Luna said. Jiro decided to fill Luna in on what happened and why they were on this mission together.

"Their scent… it's strange." Jiro said. There was no doubt that the criminals were in the building now as he and Luna spoke, but even though he could smell them, it was almost like he couldn't smell them at the same time. Was this a skill that the ninjas possessed? Jiro knew that many ninjas could hide their presence from individuals, was this power interfering with his dog senses as well?

"Any ideas on who the humans are?" Luna asked, as she began digging a hole under the gate. She wasn't too secretive about it either.

"No idea, their scent is confusing me. I know people are in there, but they are using some type of ability that is trying to trick my senses," Jiro said. He didn't want to admit this weakness of his to Luna, but he wasn't trying to withhold anything from the poodle either. "Look, I got a bad feeling about this. If anything happens, you must get out of here." Something was telling Jiro that being "dogs" were not going to help them a lot in this situation.

"Yeah, yeah. Come on! The opening should be big enough for you too!" Luna made her way to the hole that she had dug and looked over at Jiro on the other side of the fence. "You're supposed to be some sort of "ninja dog." Why are you letting me do all the work?" Luna teased. The situation they were in was too serious, so she thought that teasing Jiro a little would ease some of the tension. Jiro growled and made his way under the fence.

"I'm serious, Luna!" Jiro barked. Sighing, Luna nodded her head.

"I know," Luna said. Jiro was irritated. Luna was still not taking this as serious as she should. Jiro had been training the ninja way for many years now. Even if he was up against some talented humans, Jiro felt that he could at the very least hold off a few of them to give Luna enough time to escape. The biggest problem was if Luna would be able to do it. *I knew that I should have come alone. Luna may have some skills, but at the end of the day, she's still an ordinary dog.*

Walking ahead of Luna, Jiro waved his tail at her asking her to follow behind him. Luna grumbled a little, but complied. The two of them kept low to the ground, which wasn't difficult considering how small they were. They made sure that they were quiet as they looked for an opening to the rugged building.

"This building is so run down, surely there is some place we can slip through to get in," Jiro said irritated. He looked high and low and didn't find any opening small enough for them to move through.

"What are they discussing that's kept them in the meeting so long?" Jiro and Luna froze in their spot when they heard a male voice. They looked around but did not see anyone there.

"I don't know. Our superiors might be discussing what prophet to give those books to so that we can learn the Hakumoto Clan's special techniques." A female voice said. Jiro and Luna looked at each other confused. Who was speaking? They weren't in the dark long as smoke enveloped the space directly in front of them. When the smoke had vanished, two figures were standing in front of them.

****

"On your tummy!" Jiro whispered when the teenage human boy and girl walked closer to where Jiro and Luna were. Jiro and Luna backed up slowly, making sure that they wouldn't be stepped on. Jiro looked at the two humans again and sniffed the air around them. The female's scent wasn't familiar, but the young boy's scent matched the smell that was in Hanzo's and his house! For some reason, Jiro felt like he had smelled the boy's scent prior to the break-in, but he wasn't sure.

"I don't care what prophet they give the book to, I just want this whole process to speed up so that the prophet can decipher it and teach me the ways of the Hakumoto Clan." The boy said.

"Who says you'll be one of the ones who would learn the techniques? You're a decent ninja, but many are better." The human girl said. "You only appear like you're teleporting when you throw a smoke bomb. Hiroshi and Takashi can move that fast without being seen with just a blink of their eyes!" The boy sighed at that.

"Tsk! I should get to learn the ways of the Hakumoto Clan because Zen and I are the ones who stole the books!" Jiro and Luna listened to the two bicker for a while. Luna was bored, but Jiro absorbed all of the information that the boy and girl said. *They're fast enough to appear like they're teleporting? Even I don't know how to do that!* Jiro thought.

The two argued for a while longer, and before Jiro and Luna could blink, another human appeared in front of their eyes.

"Both of you put a sock in it!" Jiro's eyes widened at the sight of the newcomer. Despite being so young, Jiro could tell that this human boy was powerful. "Ootori-san and Monokuma-sensei are done with their meeting. They've requested that everyone meet in the main hall."

"Takashi!" the girl said. "We were just talking about you!" The girl squealed. Out of the three of them, Jiro and Luna could tell that this "Takashi" boy was more mature than the other two.
"I heard you, now meet in the main hall and stop yelling! We're ninjas, but it seems like you two are trying to bring attention to our hideout." Takashi didn't wait for the other two to answer before disappearing out of sight. The boy sighed.

"He's right. Let's go!" he said and produced a round object from his pocket. Throwing it to the ground, the area was surrounded by white smoke. When the smoke dispersed, the two humans were gone. Jiro sniffed the air to make sure. His nose was confused again, but he could definitely not smell that they were close to them any longer.

"So… is this what 'ninjas' are capable of?" Luna asked moving from her lying down position. She only saw things like teleporting on humans' television shows. She didn't know that real people could do that as well. It intrigued her, and the weight of Jiro's earlier words started to push down on her small frame. *Yes, I must be careful*, Luna thought to herself.

"Yes, though I've never seen old man Hanzo do this, I am aware that a select few ninjas are able to do this. I didn't think they'd be so young though." Jiro said shaking his head from left to right. The smoke was still disturbing his nose. "Let's go! I saw an opening over there that is big enough for the two of us to fit in." Luna nodded her head and followed Jiro's lead.

Jiro didn't know what exactly they might come against when they got inside the ninjas' hideout, but he knew for sure that this was not going to be an easy break-in even though they're dogs.

CHAPTER FIVE

"Ugh, this place is so damp on my paws," Luna groaned once she and Jiro had made it safely into the building. She was right, the floors were wet and squishy, and the smell was foul. Jiro remembered Hanzo speaking about getting prepared for any attack in any given situation, but Jiro had to admit that he didn't plan for this set-up. Still, he wasn't going to tell Luna this.

"Let's just get in and get out. Ninjas have to overcome whatever is thrown their way!" Jiro whispered.

"Humph!" Luna grumbled but kept walking forward. Jiro couldn't understand the poodle. Luna said she wanted to get out of the house and that she didn't care what they had to do, but all she was doing was complaining. If it were up to Jiro, he wouldn't be at this mysterious hide-out either, but he needed to do this for Hanzo. Hanzo meant everything to Jiro and Jiro meant everything to Hanzo. It was a terrible situation, but it had to be done.

The two dogs made their way through the large building trying their hardest to sniff out Hanzo's stolen books. It shouldn't be hard though, the books were definitely covered with Hanzo's scent. After about what seemed like hours of searching, they took a break.

"Finding these books shouldn't be this hard," Jiro said. Even if the place was ginormous and there were a lot of people in there, Jiro should have still been able to pinpoint Hanzo's books relatively fast. Was it because of the confusing scent of the place, or was his nose not as good as he thought it was?

"Maybe we need to find the main hall the humans were talking about," Luna suggested once they started moving again. "I guess that Ootori and Monokuma are their superiors. If we find where they're meeting at, we might find the books with them." Jiro trained his small body often, and he considered himself to be smart for a dog, but he'd be lying if he said that he had already thought about trying to find the main hall.

"Great thinking, Luna," Jiro reluctantly said. Jiro should have been the one to have thought about that. Maybe this uneasiness that he's feeling is clouding his judgment? At any rate, they needed to find the main hall. If Luna was right though; every ninja that is in the compound would be present. Stealing back what was stolen from them wouldn't be easy. Also, Jiro couldn't tell exactly how many people were in the building.

Looking towards the damp and dirty ground, Jiro tried to locate footprints and sniff out everyone's scent. The ninjas' smell seemed to be everywhere and nowhere at the same time, and since they were able to use their ninja arts to 'teleport' from place to place, they would more than likely not find too many footprints.

"We've been gone for quite a while, I wonder if it's getting dark yet," Luna absentmindedly said trying to make small talk. Jiro sighed. They've been gone for quite a while, but Jiro was positive that it was nowhere near dark.

"No, it's probably just now becoming afternoon," Jiro said, and the two of them froze when they heard voices in the distance. They've found them! "Stay behind me! Be quick, but don't make too much noise." Nodding quickly, Luna sped up her steps while trailing behind Jiro. Soon the two of them had made it to a main hall, and they grasped by what they saw.

There had to be about fifty powerful looking ninjas crowded together in that room.

****

"Sons and daughters," a man's powerful voice resonated throughout the room. "The time has come for us to learn the techniques of the Hakumoto!"

"Yeah," everyone in the room shouted. Jiro could tell by looking at the crowd that they were tough. Even if

Hanzo had called the police and they had gotten involved, they wouldn't have been a match for the ninjas.

"Where is it?" Luna mumbled, and Jiro was taken out of his thoughts. He looked at the white short-haired poodle and saw that her eyes scanned the crowd quickly. *Is she looking for the books*? Jiro thought and decided to do the same. Jiro was starting to think that all of his training would be no match for these capable looking ninjas.

"There!" Jiro whispered, and Luna's eyes followed his. The man who was talking, pulled out two books from thin air, another ability that these ninjas appeared to have. They'd have to watch themselves while they were in there. Jiro couldn't teleport or anything of that nature, but he could fight as well as any human.

"So how are we going to do this, Jiro?" Luna asked. Preplanning was not Jiro's specialty. He was just going to make his move when the ninjas weren't looking. "Jiro!" Luna angrily barked when Jiro didn't respond.

"Shh!" Jiro shushed Luna. He needed to focus. He wasn't close enough to the man to quietly take the books from him and run. No... he needed to get closer without people noticing him. Even as a dog, Jiro didn't think they'd just let him and Luna walk through their hideout. Unlike Jiro, these ninjas appeared to think about everything that they do.

"So... who is worthy to join us on our pilgrimage to the Prophet? Once the prophet's words reach your ears, the training and knowledge of the Hakumoto Clan will be yours!"

"Me!" many voices shouted out from the crowd.

"Monokuma-sensei bestow the honor onto me!" others began chanting throughout the hall. Their voices were making Jiro's and Luna's ears hurt. They had to do something and quick, but there weren't any openings for them to sneak in and take the books. Jiro was starting to fear the worst.

"Well, my ninja sons and daughters. Come to the stage and let me see if the book chooses you," Jiro didn't know what this Monokuma fellow was talking about, but he couldn't let anyone else lay their filthy hands on Hanzo's belongings.

"Jiro... plan?" Luna asked again this time sounding incredibly serious. She noticed that Jiro lowered his belly to the ground and a low growl started to erupt from his mouth. Whatever Jiro was thinking, Luna was sure that he wasn't organizing a safe plan. "Humph... I can read you like a book." Luna chuckled and got into her pouncing stance. It was two dogs against about fifty human ninjas. Whatever they were going to do, they had to make it work.

"No!" Jiro's loud voice exploded out of his small body, and he made a dash towards the crowd.

"What the... how did dogs get in here?" Jiro could hear a

few people asking. At first, everyone seemed confused by the charging dogs. Soon, however, the ninjas got into their own stances.

"Ryo and Zen, take care of these dogs. Everyone else, surround the building. These dogs might be police dogs scoping out the place." Monukuma said and then looked over at the man next to him. "Ootori, we must leave this place. Round up everyone after they've made sure that no cops are tailing these dogs."

"Yes sensei," The man bowed and soon the room was empty except Monukuma, Zen, Ryo, Jiro, and Luna.

"Do me proud boys, and I'll personally make sure that the Hakumoto knowledge is given to you."

The two boys nodded their heads, and Jiro finally got a good look at the human that Monukuma called Ryo. There was something vaguely familiar about him. Jiro was shaken out of his thoughts when he saw Monukuma getting ready to teleport away.

"No!" he shouted again dodging both Zen's and Ryo's attempts to block him. Monukuma slowly faced Jiro and paused. Jiro ran, jumped high in the air and did a spinning kick to knock the books out of his hand.

"What?" Monukuma questioned in surprise. He couldn't believe what he just seen a dog do.

"Kyah!" Jiro's battle cry sounded throughout the entire

room as he prepared to land another spinning kick and a chop to the man's neck. Jiro's kick couldn't connect this time, as Monukuma's aura surrounded him like a force field and made it impossible to get close enough to him.

"Take care of these dogs, they're not ordinary," Monukuma said and quickly grabbed the books. Monukuma wasted no time disappearing into thin air.

"Come back here!" Jiro shouted angrily. He had to get the books back. He needed to.

"Jiro watch out!" He heard Luna scream and Jiro looked up and froze. Moving quickly towards him was a quick and powerful kick aimed at his small frame by the mysterious Ryo!"

CHAPTER SIX

"Watch out!" Luna said as Jiro was about to be overtaken by Ryo. Luna lowered her body quickly to the ground and did a spinning kick to trip Zen and made her way over to Jiro. "Don't have your back towards the enemy!" Luna shouted and quickly got in front of Jiro and Ryo. Standing on her hind legs, Luna jumped and made two kicks and landed a punch to Ryo that knocked him down. Jiro couldn't believe his eyes.

"Luna…. you?" Jiro could barely get his words out. Luna turned to him slowly showing her sharp teeth as she smiled.

"You're not the only dog here with ninja abilities." She said. "Now help me!"

"Right!" Jiro stood next to Luna and prepared for their next strike.

"These aren't normal dogs, Zen," Ryo said looking Jiro and Luna up and down. "They have skills. Skills similar to Monukuma-sensei and Ootori-san."

"Humph, they're still dogs!" Zen said and made a bee-line towards Luna. Luna ran towards the young human and jumped up and did a cartwheel kick to the boy's chest. "Oomph!" Zen fell back onto the ground. Luna was just about to land another kick to him while he was on the floor, but he vanished in a blink of an eye.

"What are you?" Ryo asked Jiro as he attacked Jiro with all of his might. Jiro blocked and dodged Ryo's attacks to the best of his abilities while occasionally landed some strikes of his own. If Luna and Jiro were against all of the ninjas that were previously in the room, they would have lost five minutes ago. They were thankful for their battle on semi-equal grounds.

"Boy, I'm the dog that you don't want to mess with!" Jiro growled. He knew that the boy couldn't understand him, but from the looks in the young boy's eyes, it was almost as if he did understand Jiro.

"Tsk…. Retreat!" Zen said, and Ryo side glanced him. "These aren't normal dogs…. We're no match for them in our present state. Ryo, there's no time to explain. Retreat!" Ryo blocked Jiro's last punch and did several backflips away from Jiro and Zen did the same.

"You'll wish you've never interfered you little mutts!" Ryo said and threw down a smoke bomb. The smoke filled the entire room, and when it finally dispersed, Ryo and Zen were no longer there.

Jiro and Luna looked and smelled around the room. They could no longer sense anyone around them and that confusing smell of people being there and not being there at the same time was gone.

"Jiro… look." Luna said looking towards the direction where Monukuma fled. There was an old picture lying on the ground.

****

"This photo… was in one of my books. Where did you get it?" Hanzo asked when Jiro greeted him at the door to their home when the old man came back that night. Jiro couldn't tell him even if he wanted to because Hanzo wouldn't be able to understand him. The picture was a picture of Hanzo, his son Ichiro, and grandson Ryoichi from before the accident. Hanzo held the photo to his heart and cried.

Hanzo spoke to Jiro like he normally did. Hanzo wasn't hurt because the thieves took his precious books, he was sad because of the photo that was in between the pages of one of the books. This was all that he ever wanted, the picture of his family. Jiro was glad that he was able to make Hanzo happy, but that didn't satisfy him. There was still so many questions that needed to be answered.

What power do those books actually hold? What is the Hakumoto Clan's power that those ninjas are after? Why was Luna able to fight like the ninjas and like Jiro, and what about the young ninja that he fought? There was something about the young ninja Ryo that weighed heavily on his heart. Jiro knew Ryo's scent, and some of his features were familiar. Ryo the ninja and Ryoichi Hanzo's missing grandson. Were they one of the same?

Jiro was going to do whatever he needed to do to learn the truth. There were too many things that needed to be resolved, but first, he'll need to get the help from the mysterious white poodle Luna.

"This isn't over yet."

The End

CHARLIE
BOOK

Printed in Great Britain
by Amazon